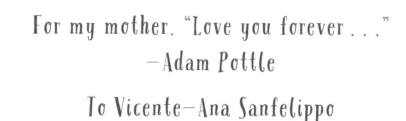

For my mother. "Love you forever . . ."
—Adam Pottle

To Vicente—Ana Sanfelippo

Reycraft Books
55 5th Avenue
New York, NY 10003
Reycraftbooks.com

Reycraft Books is a trade imprint and trademark of Newmark Learning, LLC.

Educators and Librarians our books may be purchased in bulk for promotional, educational, or business use. Please contact sales@reycraftbooks.com.

This is a work of fiction. Names, characters, places, dialogue, and incidents either are the product of the author's imagination or are used fictitiously. Any resemblance to actual persons, living or dead, is entirely coincidental.

Library of Congress Control Number: 2020908311

ISBN: 978-1-4788-6812-5

Author photo courtesy of Adam Pottle
Illustrator photo courtesy of Ana Sanfelippo

Printed in Dongguan, China. 8557/0620/17230
10 9 8 7 6 5 4 3 2 1
First Edition Hardcover published by Reycraft Books

Reycraft Books and Newmark Learning, LLC, support diversity, the First Amendment and celebrate the right to read.

The Most AWESOME CHARACTER in the World

written by Adam Pottle

illustrated by Ana Sanfelippo

Far in the distance, Philomena thought she heard a voice. She ignored it, running through the jungle.

Thick trees surrounded her, their leaves scaled like lizard skin. Their branches...

The jungle rumbled and slowly opened.
Philomena dashed through the bushes,
away from the voice. An armadillo leapt
to her side.

Dad crashed through the leaves and the jungle disappeared. Now Philomena sat, surrounded by the blanket walls of her living room fort.

"WHAT!"

Philomena shouted with her hands.

"Why aren't you wearing your hearing aids?"

"They're too loud," Philomena signed. "They distract me. I can't imagine things when I wear them."

"You need to wear them."

Dad handed her a small box. "Put them on."

Philomena growled and took the box. She
plucked out the two small hearing aids.
When she switched them on, she heard
a burst of static and clattering.

HISS!

"Is that better?"

"No!" Philomena signed. "I hate them!"

"You'll get used to them," said Dad.

Philomena shook her head.

"I don't want to wear them."

"I got this book for you," said Dad.
"The woman in the book is deaf,
 just like you."

 Philomena looked at the cover.
 The girl had a sad face.

"Try reading it," Dad said.
"After you clean up."

Philomena began putting her fort away. The blankets and chairs made loud rustling noises in her ears.

She sat on her bed and started to read. Philomena got exactly two pages into the book before she threw it at the wall.

"I can tell a way better story than that!"

Philomena turned off
her hearing aids.

"What kind of story would I write? Not something sad, like that book. Something great. Something big. Something...

AWESOME."

Philomena began drawing. She drew a figure,
then crumpled the page and threw it away. She
drew another figure, then crumpled that page.
Philomena drew and drew and drew.

And as she drew,
the room began
to change around her.

A shadow moved over her.
Philomena spun around.

The paper in Philomena's hand shook.

She held on tight as something
dragged her around the room.

Then Philomena let go,
tumbling onto her bed.

With a great rumble,

The most AWESOME CHARACTER
in the WORLD
shot off the page.

Philomena stood and held out her hand.

"Now," THE MOST AWESOME CHARACTER announced, "I demand a talent competition. Show me your talents!"

The monsters fell into line and began burping a symphony, scratching their burps on the air as they floated by.

The wheelchair heroes whizzed through the air, performing daring flips and twists.

THE MOST AWESOME CHARACTER zapped one monster with her lightning breath.

Then, with a wave of her hand, she conjured up a wrestling ring and battled against two others.

She beat them both with
a wicked, running splash.

Philomena counted,

one . . . two . . .
three!

Philomena was the last to go.

She made herself fifty feet tall and, churning the air between her hands, created a new star. She hurled it into the sky where it blazed gold and silver.

"OOH!" cheered the others.

When it was over, Philomena
collapsed onto her bed.

Dad opened the door.

"Sorry," he signed.

"Burp," Philomena signed back.

"Who's that?" Dad signed, pointing to her book.

Philomena smiled.

"The Most Awesome Writer in the World—Me."

ADAM POTTLE

Adam Pottle's writing spans several different genres. His most recent work, *The Black Drum*, is the world's first all-deaf musical and has received rave reviews from audiences and critics. His books include the memoir *Voice* and the award-winning adult novels *The Bus* and *Mantis Dreams*. Born deaf in both ears, he lives in Canada.

ANA SANFELIPPO

is from Buenos Aires, Argentina. Her work includes illustrations for books, magazines, patterns, and products. She has many published children's books and has shown her work at exhibitions in Argentina, Slovakia, England, Canada, and Spain. She combines many different hand-illustration techniques, and loves creating natural scenery and funny characters with many vibrant colors.